Tales of
Lord Su

ALSO BY I KYŪU

Lightning the Load
Confessions

Tales of Lord Su

by
I Kyūu

Poetic Justice Books
Port St. Lucie, Florida

Printed in the United States of America.
Published by Poetic Justice Books
Port Saint Lucie, Florida
www.poeticjusticebooks.com

ISBN: 978-1-950433-24-7

10 9 8 7 6 5 4 3 2

"Myth is much more important and
true than history. History is just
journalism and you know how
reliable that is."
    - Joseph Campbell

Tales of
Lord Su

Tales could be true or false. The true ones can sound false. But they are the ones we must believe. If we fail, we would no longer exist.

I Kyūu

Tale One

LORD SU CUT A PATH between two huge boulders. He made the path his home. Rain and Snow did not disturb him when he stood between the boulders. When he slept, the boulders stood ready to defend him. When he woke, the two swords he had laid on the ground would fly into their sheaths. When he left his home, the swords would fly out of their sheaths and run before him. They would warn the people and all the living things he would meet not to touch him. They said that if anyone had thoughts of hurting him, Snow and Rain would cover the land until all on it were dead.

Tale Two

LORD SU COULD CHANGE what he was. He could be an animal, a bird, or a fish. He could be an insect. He could be a male or a female. He was most dangerous when he was a girl or a woman. People would say things they shouldn't say. He would hear them. It was at those times, he would change into a monster. He could destroy their homes. He could end their lives. They would flee to new lands. There they would make new homes. They would live in fear that Lord Su would come for them.

Tale Three

LORD SU COULD TALK to all living things. This made him a loved man. This made him a feared man. He did not kill to eat. He lived off the fruit and the vegetables that fell to the ground. He drank from the water in streams, lakes, and rivers that stayed in his hands when he raised them to his lips. He was dangerous when he found that people took more than they needed. He might cut off one of their hands if they refused to listen to his warnings. He could be generous. He would stay with the poor. He would show them how they could live without the fear of not having homes or food to eat. They could live in peace. The other living things knew of his powers. They saw what he could do. They heard what he could do. They too lived in peace.

Tale Four

LORD SU LOOKED OUT on the lake. He saw his son in the water. He dipped his hand in its water. A red carp with a black circle around each eye swam up to his hand. It nibbled at Lord Su's fingers. With his other hand, Lord Su pointed to the earth in front of him. The carp jumped out of the water. It took the form of a young boy when it landed on the earth. As father and son, they turned into giant eagles. They flew to the mountain where they could see the land of the people. They looked at how the people lived. If they saw that the people lived in peace, they flew back to the lake. They turned back into Lord Su and his son, the red carp with a circle around each eye. If they saw people kill, steal, or harm others, the two eagles flew across the land. They grew in size. The earth would shake as their shadows brought darkness to the land. The people were frightened. Those who stole would return what they had taken. Those who caused harm would seek to set things right. Those who killed would beg mercy from the courts. The people would see the sky again. They saw the sun. They saw the two eagles fly across it as they flew back to their lake. The eagles turned back into Lord Su and his son, the red carp with a circle around each eye.

Tale Five

LORD SU LOOKED at the white moon and the blue sky. He saw a loon fly out of a lake. It landed on the hedges by his home. Lord Su looked up at the moon. He looked at the loon. He turned into a hawk. As the hawk flew into the air, it turned into white roses. Their petals fell on the hedges. As they turned white, the loon turned into Lord Su. He smiled at the magic of night and the role he played in it.

Tale Six

12   LORD SU SWAM in the sea. He looked at the sky. He saw a swallow dive down toward him. He smiled. When the swallow touched the water, it turned into a whale. It stayed at the surface. Lord Su climbed on its huge back. He put his arms around its hump. He whispered his hidden name. The whale rose into the air. It turned into a dragon. Lord Su smiled again. He pointed his right hand toward the land. He pointed his left hand toward the sky. The dragon flew to Lord Su's home on Mountain Bie. When they landed, the dragon turned into Falcon. It followed its master to their house. They read from Lord Su's journal. They played a game of chess. They went to sleep when they were finished. They dreamed of all they had done that day.

Tale Seven

LORD SU SPOKE to the book he had opened. He asked it to show him where they could make their new home. The book showed him the bottom of the ocean. There was a land filled with fish-like people. The book showed him the top of the mountain. There was a land filled with bird-like people. The book showed him more pages filled with more lands and people. Lord Su closed the book. He thanked it. He said they should return to their home below the mountain where they could see the ocean. They would go to other places. They would bring peace and wisdom to those who lived there. They would return to their home when they saw what they had done.

Tale Eight

LORD SU KNEW the flower. Falcon left it for him. He looked at the sky. He thanked his companion. He knew it was time to go back to the people in the land below. They needed him. He was their teacher. They learned to read the languages they spoke from him. They learned to write the words of those languages from him. They sat, listened to him play his flute. They listened to him sing. They became his students, so they could teach others to play instruments and to sing. Lord Su whistled. Falcon flew down to him. They went to the first village. He would teach them.
It was night. Lord Su entered the villagers' dreams. He left before they woke. He left for the next village. He would be their teacher as well. Falcon flew by his side. It flew back to the village where they had been.
It flew back to Lord Su before he reached the next village. It told him how well the people had learned from him.

Tale Nine

LORD SU SAW the Emperor on the wall of his City. He knew he was waiting for him. Lord Su stood on the rail of his ship. He jumped into the air. A giant squid flew out of the water. It gently caught its master with two of its tentacles. Lord Su walked up to its huge head. He sat behind it. When they reached the land, the squid spread out its arms. Lord Su walked down one of them. When he stepped on the sand, the squid became his horse. Lord Su rode up to the city. Lord Su let no people be his subjects. The people were more important than the Emperor. He was there to teach the Emperor this. His squid, his horse, were part of that teaching. He knew of a third thing that would convince the Emperor. He waved his hand from left to right. Night took the place of Day. He opened a pouch that he carried. The moon, stars, and planets fell from the sky. They grew smaller. When they reached Lord Su, they dropped into his pouch. Lord Su threw the pouch into air. It broke open. The moon, stars, and planets flew back to their places in the sky. They were their proper sizes again. Day took the place of Night. The Emperor was so frightened he promised whatever Lord Su asked him. He kept silent as Lord Su told him what he had to do. The Emperor was his people's subject. He would do what would keep peace among his people. He would do what would keep them housed and to know no hunger.

Tale Ten

16   LORD SU SAT IN the forest. He had crossed his legs. His left ankle rested on his right thigh. His right ankle rested on his left thigh. He had closed his eyes and slowed his breath. He had slowed his heart. He was ready to listen to the sounds around him. A flea and a roach were arguing. As Lord Su listened to them, he changed who he was. He was now an ant. He crawled up close to the arguers. The two insects didn't notice the ant. They were arguing about their son and their daughter. The flea's son spoke one language. The roach's daughter spoke another language. The ant excused itself. It had to ask them. It had to know if the son and the daughter knew each other. The flea and the roach laughed. They said that they knew of each other. The ant changed its size again. It was as large as a cat. It changed its size again to the size of the ant. This time a miniature Lord Su took the ant's place. He said that the children were like their parents. They were too proud. Their languages didn't help them be at peace. They kept them from being friends. The flea and the roach bowed. They knew who Lord Su was. They knew the powers he had. He could kill or change them into anything. They went off to warn their children.

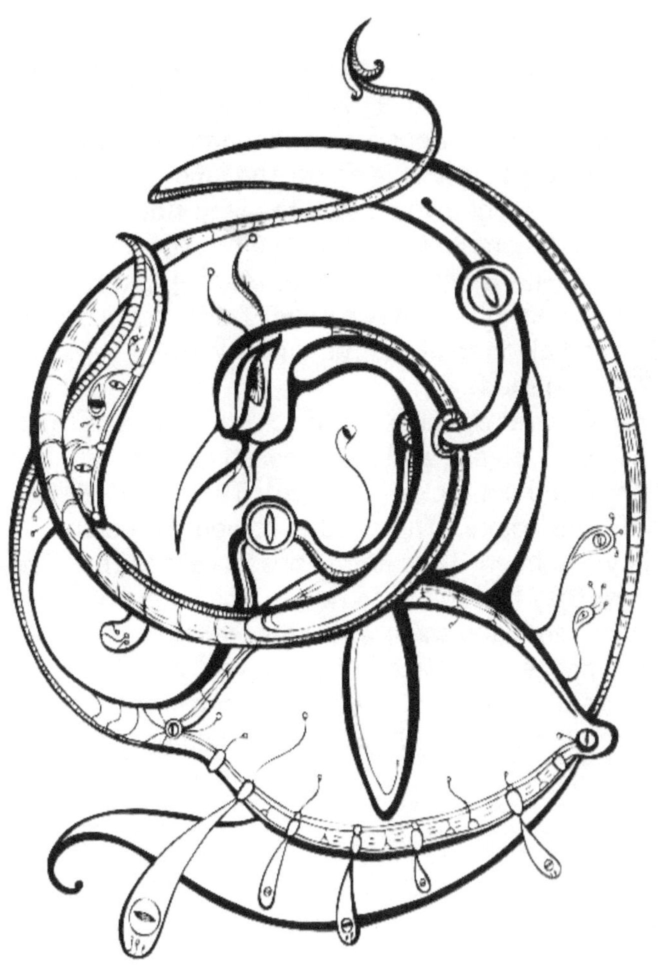

Tale Eleven

WATER SLIPPED onto the land. It was the sign for Fire. Fire spread across the land. It was the sign for Wind. Wind swept across the land. It was the sign for Lord Su to ride across the land. Falcon flew by his side. The two crossed the land slowly. The hooves of Lord Su's horse left new earth where they passed. The wings of Falcon left new grasses, trees, and flowers where they passed. This is how Lord Su and Falcon renewed the lands. Water, Fire, and Wind vanished.

Mountains, valleys, and forests looked as they had. Seas, rivers, and lakes looked as they had. People did not look as they had. Their hands were different colors. Their bodies stayed the colors they had been. They knew Lord Su caused this. They knew they had to live in peace. The colors of their hands reminded them what they had done before the change. Lord Su and Falcon went back to their mountain. They looked down on their work. They were pleased. They hoped they would not have to do it again.

Tale Twelve

LORD SU missed his son. He asked Falcon to fly to Lake Ie. It was in the valley far from Mount Bie. His son lived in it as a red carp with a black circle around each eye. Lord Su told Falcon to say what they had done to the lands. That he had not wanted to cause him trouble. Falcon flew to the lake. It dipped a talon in the water as Lord Su had once put a hand in the lake. The red carp saw the talon. It jumped out of the water and landed by Falcon.

"Falcon, my father and you did not cause me trou-ble. I knew when Water rushed onto the land what would happen. I dreamt that Father shrunk all the fish, animals, birds, and insects. He swept them up to Mount Bie. He took out a pouch. He untied the pouch. He held it open. The fish, animals, birds, and insects dropped into it. They were safe there while Water, Fire, and Wind brought havoc to the land."

Falcon bowed its head. It said it would speak with Lord Su. It would tell him what the son dreamed. It would tell him he had not caused a problem for you.

Tale Thirteen

LORD SU took out his looking glass. He looked out across the land. He saw ten statues of a huge horse and its rider at points around a town. He was curious. He spun around with his arms held straight out from his sides. When he stopped, he looked like an old man. He asked Falcon to come with him. Falcon spread out its wings. It spun around. When it stopped, it looked like a hunting dog. Lord Su and Falcon were ready. They would see who carved the statues. They would learn why the statues were made. They left for the town. A story was there. And they wanted to hear it.

I will not tell you of Lord Su and Falcon's journey to the statues. They would not want you to know all the changes they made on the way. It would reveal too much about them. But, I can tell you the story they heard.

When the old man and his dog stood by the statue at the city's gate, ten carvers came out to them. Their leader stepped forward. He looked at the old man. "You are Lord Su and Falcon who saved us." Lord Su was not surprised. He turned back to his old self. Falcon did the same.

Lord Su sat on the ground with his legs crossed in a full lotus. He waved his hands in front of him. Ten sitting blankets drifted down the sky. They landed in front of him and Falcon. Lord Su pointed to them and invited the carvers to sit. When they sat with their legs crossed in full lotuses, a pitcher of wine and a plate of cheese appeared before all ten. That was not all. Glasses, knives, and cloth napkins also drifted down from the sky. The glasses appeared before the right hand of each of the carvers. The knives and the napkins appeared before each carver's left hand.

The leader of the carvers spoke:

At one time we were bandits. We had raided Kawa in the West and had come back with all the treasures we could carry. We heard a horse bay outside our tent. We went to check if it was one of ours. There, we saw a Stranger dressed in black sitting on a black horse.

"I've come for the treasure you stole," the Stranger called out. "And to punish you."

"You're in my camp," our leader said. "I'm the one who tells others what to do." He signaled for us to surround the stranger. We waited for the order to attack.

"Don't move, or I'll turn you to stone," the Stranger said. He spoke softly, but we all heard him. The Stranger and the horse were the biggest we had ever seen. The horse had deep red eyes. They were the color of the fires we made to warm ourselves on cold nights. The Stranger's voice seemed to carry the wind. Each word seemed as if it were a gust of wind. We felt colder and colder.

One of us spoke. "You, who has the voice of the wind, what are you called?"

"I am Lord of the North Winds. I am not pleased with what you did to the people in Kawa."

"Why should you care for them?" answered our leader. "Kawa is in the West. You are of the North. You have nothing to do with us."

"I do! My wife, the mother of my children, comes from there. When you bring sadness to her, you anger me."

Our leader signaled us to attack the Stranger. With the first step we took, his horse closed its eyes. The Stranger blew on his fingers. He pointed at us. We turned to stone.

He spoke to us. "If you want to live, give up your leader. I will hear you. I will hear your promise behind your stone lips. Choose now. Will you stay stones or turn back to men?"

We promised we would give up our leader. We said we would return what we had taken from Kawa. With our promise, we turned back to men. We gave up our leader. We loaded ten horses with the treasures we had taken.

"Now, do as you said you would," ordered the Stranger. We tied our leader's hands behind him. We turned him over to the Stranger, the one who called himself the Lord of the North Winds.

The Stranger pulled on the reins of his horse. It blew air through its mouth. The air felt warm. "I will give you the skill to become carvers of stone. You will make beautiful stone figures and jewelry. Everyone will want them. You won't need to steal. But if you ask too much for your creations, I will turn you back to stone. A black cloud will come from the North. You will not be able to hide from it. When it touches you, you will turn to stone.

The Lord of North Winds turned his horse
toward Kawa. He rode off. We became carvers of
stone. The first things we carved were the small
statues we wear around our necks. Each statue was
of the Stranger with the horse that he rode. Next,
we carved the ten statues that brought you here.

The leader of the carvers stood up. The nine
other carvers stood up. Lord Su and Falcon stood up.
They bowed. They thanked the carvers. The carvers
bowed. They thanked Lord Su and Falcon. Lord Su
and Falcon then visited each of the ten statues.
Then they could not be seen.

When Lord Su and Falcon were back at their
home on Mount Bie, they knew what they would do
next. They would find the Stranger and his horse.
They knew they would find a pair with similar
powers to those they had.

Lord Su and Falcon sat in a full lotus. They
did not eat nor did they drink. They did not sleep.
They quieted their breathing. For the ten statues
and their ten carvers, they sat that way until on the
tenth day Falcon rose. It used the talons on one its
feet to write it had found where they could find the
Stranger and its horse. Lord Su smiled. He too had
found the answer. Now, he was sure it was the right
answer.

Tale Fourteen

WHEN LORD SU stood before the Lord of the East, he was greeted by a woman dressed as he was. She had a falcon next her. It was as large as the one Lord Su had. Falcon dropped out of the sky and landed next to Lord Su. Falcon spoke for Lord Su. It asked what the woman was called.

She answered, "I am called Lord Su. My Lady or My Queen doesn't sound right to my people."

Lord Su smiled. He asked the Lord Su of the East what her falcon was called. She, too, smiled and answered, "Falcon as your Falcon is. I know why you came. I will tell you what you want to know. First, you must listen to my story. Second, you must tell me if you liked it, or how I can make it better."

Lord Su looked at Falcon. They both bowed. Falcon spoke again. It said it knew Lord Su would agree with her request. "Lord Su and I will listen to your story. And he will do as you say."

The Lord of the East pointed to the ground. Four purple carpets appeared before the Su's and two Falcons. Each sat on one. Lord Su began her story:

> Long ago, a tribe of bears lived in a temple at the top of a mountain between two countries. The rulers of these countries had been childhood friends. Then one of them stole the pouch the other had used to hold his coloring sticks. They stopped being friends on that day. When they

became rulers of their countries, they began to fight each other. The bears became involved in the kings' fight since their armies used the mountain to get into the other's land. They had less time to care for their gardens and to study their books. When the rulers and their soldiers crossed into each other's countries, they didn't stop at the temple. On the way back, they would leave their wounded for the bears to look after. The bears not only had to care for the wounded soldiers, but they had to keep them from fighting with each other.

The two rulers fought for ten years. In the tenth year, the ruler, whose pouch had been stolen, crossed into his enemy's country. He took a small group of solders with him. They set fire to the fields below the mountain. Its ruler with a group of his soldiers chased after his enemy. The two rulers met up near the mountain pass. They fought each other. They were badly wounded. They had to stay at the temple while recovering. Before the rulers could stay at the temple, the leader of the bears made them promise to stop fighting.

Knowing that they would die if they couldn't stay with the bears, the rulers gave into his demands. They signed three scrolls. They agreed to keep a peace between them. The bears sent one scroll to each of the rulers' people announcing their agreement. The bears kept the third scroll. They had the rulers play chess with each other while staying with them. They had the rulers promise to play with each other when they healed and returned to their own countries.

When the two rulers healed, they returned to their own countries. They kept their word because the leader of the bears had threatened that they would destroy their temple. He said they would go to a distant land. The rulers knew they would lose all the knowledge the bears had kept. They knew they wouldn't be able to go to them when they were ill. The rulers still hated each other. As they had promised, they still played chess with each other. It seemed the more they played with each other the less they wanted to fight. One day the ruler who had stolen the small pouch holding the coloring sticks returned it to his childhood friend. Then peace came to their two lands.

Lord Su got up. He bowed to Lord Su of the East. He said, "I have nothing to add to your story. I know I might meet another Lord Su. He or she will be the Lord of the North. Like us, this Lord will have powers and a story for me. This one will answer the question I first sought at the city of the ten statues.

Tale Fifteen

LORD SU and Falcon knew they would need to find a way to go to the home of the Lord of the North. Lord Su stood with his arms stretched out from his sides. Falcon did the same thing with its wings. It became a second Lord Su.

The two of them spun around. They spun faster and faster. They turned into two whirlwind-like clouds. They flew across their own land. They flew across the land of the East and of the South. When they reached the Land of the North, they slowed their spinning. They landed next to a seated Lord of the North.

The Lord of the North sat silently. He saw the two clouds turn back to Lord Su and Falcon. He told them to sit with him. "Sit here. Hear my story. It is a long story. When it is finished, you will have questions. I will not answer them. The story has its own answers. When you return to your own land, you will know them. What you do after that will come from those answers.

"For now listen to my story:

Wood Boy and his father made big canoes so their people could cross the ocean. Wood Boy dreamed of going down river. One day he asked his father if they could make a small canoe.

"Son, why do you want us to make a small canoe?"

"I want to take it down river, Father."

"Why down river?" the father asked.

"To see the Rock People."

Wood Boy's father picked up a small rock and drew a canoe on the ground with it. He had not seen the rocks that looked like people, but he had heard people talk about them. He said they would begin building the canoe in two days. Then he asked Wood Boy, "What will you do after you see the Rock People?"

"Come back with a good story!"

"Yes, your grandmother would like that!"

Building a small canoe was not the same as building a big one. It had to be light as well as strong. Wood Boy would need to pull it onto the shore when he reached the land of the Rock People. The canoe's frame was made from a lighter wood than they used for big canoes. The paddles were made from the same wood. The canoe's skin came from tree bark. Wood Boy and his father put the bark in a large net and let it soak in a lake for two days. On the third day, they pulled out the net and wrapped the softened bark around the canoe's frame.

The father put his hands on the canoe. "It needs to dry. Let's visit your grandmother, Wood Boy. She'll name your canoe."

Wood Boy's grandmother was their people's storyteller. The father knew she would name the canoe well. Wood Boy and he went to their home where they washed before picking out some flowers from their garden for the grandmother.

The grandmother was sitting in a chair on her porch. When she saw them with flowers for her, she smiled. "Son and son of my son, thank you for the flowers. What can I help you with?"

"Grandmother to my son and mother to me, we come for your help. We need you to name his canoe."

"Wood Boy," she asked, "why have you built a canoe?"

"So I can go down river, Grandmother."

"Then, Grandson, let us call it 'The Finder of Stories.'" She smiled and told her grandson he would tell his stories when he came back from the rocks that looked like people.

Wood Boy asked his grandmother how she knew he wanted a canoe to find the Rock People. She laughed. "When your father was your age, he too wanted to go down river. He too wanted to find the Rock People. That's why he helped you."

The small canoe was named well. When Wood Boy came back, he had a good story to tell. One no one had heard before.

He said he was on the river for five days.

"Every evening I paddled over to the shore. I pulled the canoe onto the land. I put up my small tent and made a fire. I threw my line in the water and caught a fish. After cleaning it, I looked for vegetables to cook. If I found some, I put them and the fish in the fire. After eating, I wrote in my journal and checked the stars to see how far I had gone that day.

"In the morning, I picked fruits and ate them

with the seed bread mother had made for the trip. I cleaned up and started on my journey for that day.

"On the fifth day, I saw the rocks that looked like people. I paddled over to the shore. I dragged my canoe onto the beach in front of the rocks. I walked around them many times.

"I thought I saw one of the rocks move. For three days, I sat on the ground waiting to see if I was right.

"An old man came up to me on the third day. He asked if I could sit without thinking. I laughed.

"He hit his forehead with the palm of one of his hands. He sat down next to me and told me a story of Cricket Man.

"'Cricket Man loved food. He was always eating or looking for food. He even dreamed of being food.

'One day he even turned into food. His fingers and toes turned into carrots. His arms and legs and his hands and feet turned into cow and pig bones. The skin of yams covered them. His face turned into the white meat of coconuts. His eyes turned into blue berries. His ears turned into pears. His lips and tongue turned into red chili peppers. His hair and eyebrows turned into parts of spinach leaves. His trunk turned into a squash.'"

Wood Boy laughed. He said, "That was the old man's story."

His grandmother laughed too. She asked what happened next.

"I said, 'I hope Cricket Man didn't get hungry.

He didn't start to eat himself.'

The old man laughed. He didn't stop laughing. The more he laughed the more he looked like Rock People. When he stopped laughing, I saw a rock man."

Wood Boy's grandmother loved his story. She told it to everyone she could. They loved the story too, but they didn't know what it meant.

This didn't stop Wood Boy. He kept making trips in his small canoe. It didn't stop his grandmother, either.

Each time Wood Boy came back, she asked what happened on his trip. Of course, she told everyone what Wood Boy told her. Some of his stories were very strange and difficult to understand. His stories were very strange but all those who heard them knew what they meant.

The Lord of the North stood up. He said, "It's time for the two of you to go back to your home."

Lord Su stood up. He raised his arms from his sides. Falcon did the same thing with its wings. It became a second Lord Su.

The two of them spun around. They spun faster and faster. They turned into two whirlwind-like clouds. They flew across the lands. When they reached their own land, they slowed their spinning. They landed on Mount Bie. They again became Lord Su and Falcon.

Tale Sixteen

THEY TALKED of him as if he were a God. Lord Su would walk away. He would come back as a scholar or a monk. He would ask them what they believed in. He never asked who was their God. They could not help themselves. After they spoke of God, they would add his name to that of God. Lord Su would ask if they had more than one God. Those that would answer yes were stuck. Lord Su would laugh. He would turn into an eagle. Then he became a wolf or a dog. When he turned back to Lord Su, he would bow. He would say that he could be many things. But he could not be a God.

34

about the author

I Kyūu is a spiritual explorer with a
great interest in folk tales and myth
and the origins of language.

afterword

A Tale of I Kyūu
by Kris Haggblom

A while ago, a strange little book appeared in our local bookstore. *Lord Su (Ten Tales of Who He Was)*, with its vaguely oriental-looking cover art was filled with the adventures of a mysterious creature named Lord Su, occasionally joined by a familiar in the form of a falcon or dancing swords. Lord Su would sweep down from a mountain stronghold to interact with people, emperors, fish, books, all manner of creation, impart some knowledge or life-lesson, then return home and contemplate the outcome. Were these fairytales? retellings of ancient myths? Whatever they were, they were intriguing to say the least and left the reader with a breathless sense of wonder.

As if by some magic, perhaps one of Lord Su's spells, a second book appeared with more tales. *More Tales of Lord Su* was graced with a cover image that was somewhere between cuddly alien and "does it bite." This time we learned that Lord Su and Falcon's home is named Mount Bie, met numerous alternate versions of Lord Su as did Lord Su – an astounding version of "Lord Su, I would like to introduce you to Lord Su" – and we were treated to an intricate web of tales within tales within tales.

original cover of the first Lord Su book

original cover of the second Lord Su book

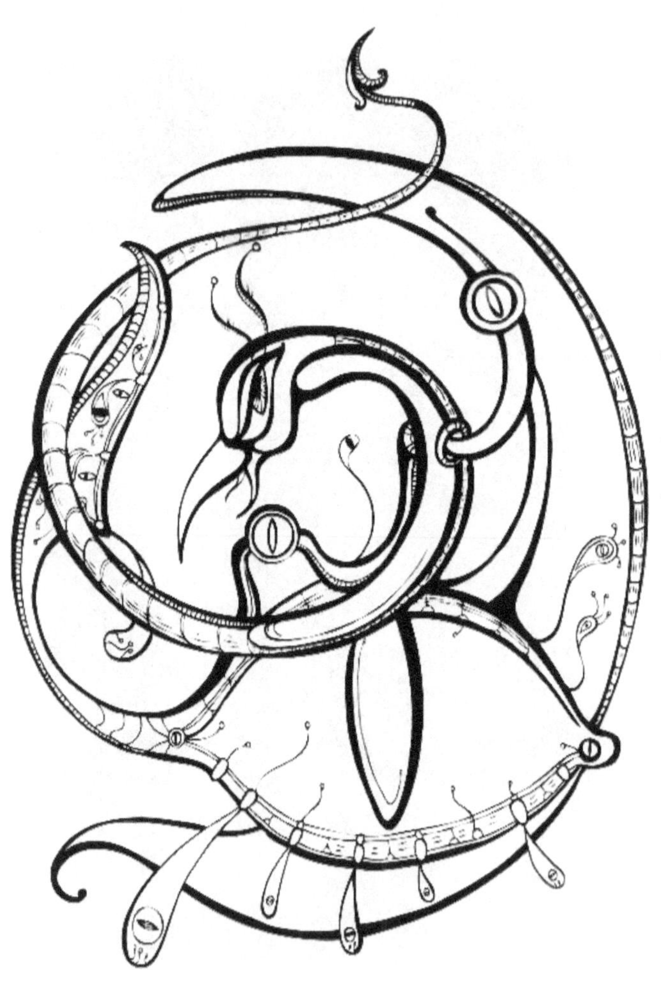

the last page of the first Lord Su book

Both of these limited print run books are out of print and difficult, I'd daresay impossible, to find. So, when a chance meeting with I Kyūu occurred early this year, I seized upon the opportunity to bring these tales to a wider audience. The book in your hands is the result of that meeting – bringing together the two earlier collections in a single volume.

These are stories that completely transcend genre. The reader is an essential part of the writing, drawing on their own philosophy and experience and forming a picture unique to each encounter. No two people will see these tales the same way. I Kyūu has crafted a world apart.

colophon

Tales of Lord Su, by I Kyūu,
was set with TREBUCHET and CALIBRI fonts
by SpiNDec, Port Saint Lucie, Florida
The jacket and covers were designed by
Kris Haggblom, Port Saint Lucie, Florida